The Grumpy Bunny
Joins the Team

by Justine Korman

illustrated by Lucinda McQueen

WHISTLESTOP®

Troll

P9-DEH-189

Nakayuna Central Schools

191128

To everybunny who wasn't picked first.
It's never too late to play your best!
—J.K.

To Jada and Bun bun,
the best ballplayers on Denny Hill!
Love, Lucy

Text copyright © 1998 by Justine Korman.
Illustrations copyright © 1998 by Lucinda McQueen.

Published by WhistleStop, an imprint and registered trademark
of Troll Communications L.L.C.

Grumpy Bunny is a trademark of Justine Korman, Lucinda McQueen,
and Troll Communications L.L.C.

All rights reserved. No part of this book may be reproduced or utilized in any form
or by any means, electronic or mechanical, including photocopying,
recording, or by any information storage and retrieval system, without
written permission from the publisher.

Printed in the United States of America.
ISBN 0-8167-4543-9

10   9   8   7   6   5   4   3   2   1

After a long day of teaching, Hopper the grumpy bunny was ready to go home. But his friend Coach needed to talk.

"The big baseball game between Easter Bunny Elementary and Swamp Cabbage Primary is coming up," Coach said with a sigh. "They don't call those skunks the Invincible Stinkers for nothing. They always win! And I just don't have enough time to coach our whole team by myself."

The grumpy bunny frowned. He didn't like the sound of this conversation!

Hopper had never been good at baseball. He'd tried to play when he was just a schoolbunny, but he was always the worst player on his team. He couldn't throw, field, or hit.

At the big play-off, little Hopper struck out in the final inning and lost the game for his team! The next season, he wasn't even asked to play. And some of Hopper's friends wouldn't talk to him anymore.

Coach slapped Hopper on the shoulder and brought him back to the present. "So what do you say, pal? Will you help the team? Will you be my assistant coach?"

Hopper thought hard. "Why don't you ask Marigold?" Coach's sweetheart, Marigold, was the girls' gym coach.

"Her track team is training for a big meet," Coach explained. Then he added, "Lilac will be assisting Marigold."

Hopper's ears perked up when he heard Lilac's name. The grumpy bunny adored the pretty music teacher.

"We practice Mondays and Wednesdays after school," Coach said, without waiting to hear Hopper's answer. "See you tomorrow on the field." He tossed a baseball cap at Hopper.

Hopper's paws slapped together. The cap dropped at his feet. Hopper sighed and thought, *What have I gotten myself into this time?*

The grumpy bunny found out at practice the next day.

"I'm going to coach the starting lineup," Coach told him. "I need you to work with Skip, Flip, and Trip."

As Coach led the rest of the team away for drills, Hopper looked at the three bunnies left on the bench.

"We're hopeless," Trip said quietly.

Hopper smoothed the brim of his cap. What would Coach say? "You're not hopeless. Be hopeful! If you try your hardest, you're bound to improve."

"We couldn't get any worse," Flip pointed out.

Skip giggled shyly.

Hopper smiled. "From now on, you're Hopper's Hopefuls," he said encouragingly.

But the grumpy bunny soon found that it takes more than hope to hit a ball. It takes aim, skill, strength—and the ability to move without tripping over your own paws!

Hopper tried hard not to get mad at Trip when she tripped. He gritted his teeth when Skip dodged a pitch and when Flip flopped.

"Let's practice some fielding instead," he suggested.

But the Hopefuls' fielding was even worse than their batting! Flip took forever to reach the ball. Trip tripped over first base. And Skip ran away as if the ball were going to bite him!

Finally, the grumpy bunny couldn't take any more. He threw down his cap. He was about to say "I quit!" when he heard the sound of singing from the girls' field.

Hopper saw Lilac leading the relay team. The runners were singing a round while passing the baton.

Lilac waved. She left the bunny-runners to their practice and came over to say hello.

"Why are they singing?" Hopper asked curiously.

"I think singing helps the runners work smoothly together in rhythm," Lilac explained. "That way they'll learn to run as a team."

Hopper's ears twitched with sudden excitement. "As a team . . ." he repeated thoughtfully.

Hopper returned to his Hopefuls. "From now on, forget about baseball," he told them. "Our goal is to become a team, and that means using our strengths to help each other."

"What if we don't have any strengths?" Skip asked.

"Everyone's good at something," Hopper assured him. "For instance, you're good at avoiding the ball. So you can lead us in a dodgeball game."

With Skip's help, Flip learned to move faster, and Trip stopped tripping over her feet!

Flip was good at juggling. So Hopper said, "Let's teach
these bunnies how to catch."

At first, Skip was afraid of the falling balls. But after
a while, he stopped flinching and started catching!

Trip had a tougher time. But she kept trying!

"Now let's juggle together," Hopper decided.
The bunnies put on their baseball gloves and began
to toss a ball. Flip, Skip, and Trip had always done poorly
during catching practice. But this seemed different. They
were playing—and having a good time!

Hopper noticed Coach's group running laps. He tapped Trip's arm and cried, "Tag! You're it!"

The grumpy bunny raced away. Trip took off after him. She was so caught up in the game, she forgot to trip over her feet. Instead, she tagged Flip, who started chasing Skip!

A little while later, Coach blew his whistle to signal the end of practice.

Hopper sighed. "I wish we had more time." The grumpy bunny couldn't believe what he'd just said. But it was true. He'd been having fun!

Trip agreed. "This was more like a party than a workout!" she exclaimed.

That gave Hopper another idea . . .

At the next practice, Hopper's Hopefuls played party
games. They started with "hot potato."

"Faster!" Hopper shouted.

The Hopefuls threw the "potato" baseball faster and faster.

Eventually, they were going so fast, they could barely see
the ball. But no one dropped it!

Next Hopper brought out a piñata. "Remember, work as a team," he said. "The Hopefuls who aren't blindfolded can help the other one bat."

"What kind of candy is inside?" Flip wondered.

"There's candy inside?" Skip asked excitedly as he took hold of the bat.

With that, Skip swung harder than he ever thought he could.

THA-WACK! The piñata burst open in a shower of sweets.

Skip happily shared the candy with the rest of the team. Hopper was *very* proud of his Hopefuls.

On the morning of the big game, Hopper's phone rang.

"It's me," a voice croaked.

The grumpy bunny knew who it was. He just didn't want to believe it.

"I'm sick," Coach wheezed. "I can't help our team beat the Invincible Stinkers."

"You can't give up now!" Hopper protested. "The team is counting on you!"

"No, the team is counting on *you*," Coach rasped.

"What?!" Hopper squeaked.

"You can do it!" Coach said. "You'll be great. Good luck!"
And he hung up the phone.

Hopper's stomach flip-flopped as he muttered to himself,
"Here's another fine mess I've gotten myself into."

At the ball field, the grumpy bunny's stomach was still full of butterflies as he watched the seats fill up with fans. *We're going to lose,* he thought nervously.

Just then, Lilac arrived. She saw right away that Hopper was worried.

"You'll be fine," the pretty bunny said in a soothing voice. "Just do your best."

Inspired by Lilac's confidence, Hopper nodded. "We'll play our best—as a team!" he said enthusiastically.

Craig Media Center
2566 Balltown Road
Niskayuna, N.Y. 12309

At that moment, Casey the catcher ran up. "Pete, Sandy, and Babe have Coach's flu. They can't play. We'll never win without our three best players."

Hopper's ears drooped. The team was doomed!

Then he saw his Hopefuls waiting eagerly on the bench. "Every bunny is a 'best player,'" Hopper declared. "With Trip, Skip, and Flip, we'll do fine." He winked at the Hopefuls as he took out some baseballs. "Now get out there and toss those potatoes!"

Hopper's Hopefuls played well through the whole game. Trip tripped in the outfield, but she juggled the ball into her glove.

"Go, team, go!" the bunnies cheered.

Flip almost got tagged out at second base. But he quickly used one of Skip's dodgeball moves.

"Safe!" the umpire shouted.

"Yeah, team!" the fans cried.

The score was tied in the last inning. The bunnies had two outs. The crowd was tense. Who would win?

Timid Skip was at bat. He looked scared.

Hopper paced. "Do it for the team!" he called.
Then he added, "Pretend it's a piñata!"

Skip swung the bat so hard, he sent the ball
sailing out of the park!

Easter Bunny Elementary had won the game!

Suddenly, Hopper felt himself being lifted up until he rode on a bobbing mass of shoulders. Cheers rang out all around. Lilac smiled at him. Hopper had never felt less grumpy in his entire life!

Sir Byron, the Great Hare, came down from the stands to shake Hopper's paw. "Excellent game!" he said. "You're a good bunny to have on the team."

The grumpy bunny's ears perked up. He looked over at his Hopefuls and grinned. Hopper had finally made the team!

It's not how many flies you catch
or times you cross home plate.
Teamwork and togetherness
make every player great!